CHOOSE YOUR OWN A...

NINJA CYBORG

BY JAY LEIBOLD

ILLUSTRATED BY TOM LA PADULA

An R. A. Montgomery Book

BANTAM BOOKS
NEW YORK • TORONTO • LONDON • SYDNEY • AUCKLAND

RL 4, age 10 and up

NINJA CYBORG
A Bantam Book / January 1995

CHOOSE YOUR OWN ADVENTURE® *is a registered*
trademark of Bantam Books,
a division of Bantam Doubleday Dell Publishing Group, Inc.
Registered in U.S. Patent and Trademark Office and elsewhere.

Original conception of Edward Packard

Cover art by Romas Kukalis
Interior illustrations by Tom La Padula

ISBN 0-553-56395-5

Published simultaneously in the United States and Canada

Bantam Books are published by Bantam Books, a division of
Bantam Doubleday Dell Publishing Group, Inc. Its trademark,
consisting of the words "Bantam Books" and the portrayal of a
rooster, is Registered in U.S. Patent and Trademark Office and in
other countries. Marca Registrada. Bantam Books, 1540 Broadway,
New York, New York 10036.

PRINTED IN THE UNITED STATES OF AMERICA
OPM   0 9 8 7 6 5 4 3 2

NINJA
CYBORG

WARNING!!!

Do not read this book straight through from beginning to end! These pages contain many different adventures you may have as a ninja studying martial arts with your friend Nada. From time to time as you read along, you will be asked to make a choice. The choices you make will determine whether you succeed or fail in tracking down the mysterious presence that has invaded a ninja mountain retreat.

As you search for clues, you will learn more about the secret and sometimes magical world of the ninja. You may even have to go into the future to solve the mystery! You are responsible for your fate because *you* make the decisions. After you make a choice, follow the instructions to find out what happens to you next.

Be careful. The ninja of the future may be deadly! To learn more about the ninja, read the Special Note on the next page. You can also look up unfamiliar words in the Glossary.

Good luck!

SPECIAL NOTE ON THE NINJA

The ancient art practiced by the ninja is called *ninjutsu.* It was developed in the eleventh and twelfth centuries by Japanese mountain clans. They drew on mystical wisdom, martial arts expertise, and special tactical knowledge to refine the new discipline. Their art was passed on secretly from one generation to the next.

Each *ryu,* or school, has its own specialty. A student may learn about empty-hand combat, special weapons and devices, means of escape, deception, and invisibility, and the strategies of espionage, attack, and defense.

The most important aspect of the martial arts is the discipline of daily practice. A student will meditate and practice basic exercises over and over until they are part of his or her everyday life. After many years of training, the student may be able to "forget" this training and achieve a state of emptiness, which is also a state of complete awareness and readiness.

According to legend, mountain creatures called *tengu* first taught the ninja their art. They also taught them *kuji,* or ninja sorcery. This is used to channel energy and key into the underlying forces of the universe, perhaps even to alter the fabric of space and time.

GLOSSARY

Cyborg—Cybernetic organism: a humanoid similar to a robot but made from organic as well as mechanical parts.

Dojo—The place where martial arts are practiced.

Gi—A loose-fitting cotton outfit worn while practicing martial arts.

Kaginawa—A grapple or hook attached to the end of a rope.

Kami—A spirit, demon, or deity.

Kuji—Ninja sorcery, sometimes described as "nine hands cutting"; mystic finger positions are used to channel energy and change the fabric of reality.

Kusari-fundo—A weapon consisting of a length of chain with weights at either end.

Kusari-gama—A weapon made up of a blade attached to a chain.

Ninja—A student of the art of ninjutsu.

Ninjutsu—Called "the art of stealth" or "way of invisibility." An unconventional discipline combining martial arts, special weapons, techniques of secrecy, and sorcery.

Ryu—A school or tradition of a martial art.

Saiminjutsu—Ninja hypnotism or trance.

Sakki—"The force of the killer"; a kind of sixth sense that allows ninja to detect harmful intentions.

Sensei—Teacher or master in the martial arts.

Shuko—Steel claws worn on the hands or feet.

Shuriken—Deadly ninja throwing blades, often star shaped.

Tengu—Mythical creatures said to have first taught the ninja their art. They are shown as old men with long noses or beaks, wings, and claws. They live in trees in the mountains and are said to be the condensed principle of *yin*, or darkness.

You think you're just about to achieve perfect peace. It's taken over a week to get to this point, but you're almost there.

Your surroundings are falling away from you: the straw mat under your crossed legs, the cedar slats of the tiny meditation house, the fragrant breeze wafting through the window, the quaking leaves of the birch and cryptomeria trees, the plunging valleys and peaks on all sides of the Kurayama family mountain retreat. Almost nothing remains but your sense of inner calm— and your friend Nada Kurayama.

Nada is sitting cross-legged next to you, wrapped in her own meditation. She seems to be able to reach a quiet state much more quickly than you. This is a surprise, considering what an impatient person she is. Her parents knew what they were in for when she was born. Her name in Japanese means "the rough, open part of the sea where navigation is difficult."

But right now she's motionless as a stone. At first you were envious that she disappeared into tranquility so much more easily than you. Then you remembered that she grew up in a ninja family. She's been practicing meditation for years.

Turn to page 2.

Anyhow, you're not supposed to compare yourself to others. What's important is your own progress. That's why you and Nada decided to take this two-week retreat into the mountains. And now that you've stopped trying so hard, you're finally about to reach the state of nothingness you've been seeking for days.

Except—something is wrong. Something has *changed*. The silence is a little *too* silent. The breeze has mysteriously died. The pulse of the insects outside is different.

Is this just a trick your stupid mind is playing on you? During the hours of meditation leading up to this moment, you discovered all the tricks your mind can play to keep you from reaching what seems like a very simple state: complete silence. If it wasn't thinking about food, it was chattering about your next chore, or repeating some idiotic jingle, or just tripping over itself trying not to think about not trying to think about anything.

After several days of this you finally realized why the sensei calls the mind "stupid."

"Your body has a deep intelligence," he said. "But all the noise of the modern world makes you forget it. The mind gets filled up with irrelevant matters and becomes stupid. Unless you are lucky enough to be born and raised away from all this, you must work for years to unlearn it. Then you can recover that simple but deep intelligence."

Turn to page 40.

He waves his hands in front of him. "Oh, no, no! That's no place for me! This is for you, the young ones, to solve." Then his face darkens. "But it is true that if this ninja succeeds in putting the scroll to use, then more than just the secrecy of our *ryu* is at stake. The future itself will be in peril."

Nada turns to you, awaiting your go-ahead. But you don't know if you want to give it. The future seems a terribly frightening and dangerous place. Shouldn't you try every other avenue before plunging into it?

If you agree to go into the future, turn to page 53.

If you're not ready to go into the future yet, turn to page 114.

Your premonition is just too strong to resist. "Nada, something is happening," you say.

Nada's head jerks in your direction. She doesn't question your intuition for a moment. "Where?" she asks, snapping into business mode.

"Outside," you say. "Down the hill."

Together you climb down from the small, clean, empty pagoda that sits at the highest point of the mountain retreat. Now that you're moving, you have a hard time getting a fix on the source of the problem. "It's more like something's missing," you explain to Nada. "The pulse of the crickets changed, or the air stopped moving for a minute."

"Hmm," she says. She pauses, listening. "I don't sense *sakki*—or any human presence at all."

"Me neither," you admit. "Let's look in the main house."

You and Nada go down the path to the main building. The compound is made up of a number of structures artfully placed among trees and gardens on the mountainside. The main one is a modest house with a kitchen, living room, and several small sleeping rooms. Other buildings house the library, dojo, workshop, garden tools, and ninja implements.

Everything is very simple. The purpose of the place is to provide a minimum amount of comfort while practitioners retreat from their daily lives to spend time in contemplation or to learn *kuji*—ninja sorcery.

Turn to page 77.

"Kurayama," Richard mutters after Nada gives her name. "Yeah, I've seen that name around here. This used to be your family's place, huh? Hope you don't mind me camping out. I just blitzed out of the Miasma as soon as I could get my hands on a PTV. That was about a year ago. Hacked my way past the laser-wave security field and found the place just like it is now. How'd *you* escape the Miasma?"

"What's the Miasma?" you ask.

Richard squints hard at you. "You from off-planet or *what*?"

"Oh, I'm from this planet," you reply casually. "Fifty years ago."

"Whoa, that's hyper!" Richard responds. "You're into time-shifting, then?" When you hesitate, he goes on, "I've heard rumors of a time-shifting device being invented, ever since astrophysics allowed us to bar code our exact eleven-dimensional site in the space-time continuum. See, there might be a way to recode it for a new time-space location in the past—or future. However, the means-of-transport technology is fuzzy."

Seeing that all this means nothing to you, he examines you more closely. "How *did* you get here, anyway?"

Nada gives the simplest answer. "*Kuji.* Ninja sorcery."

"*Right*," Richard says dubiously.

Turn to page 83.

"Oh yes it will," Monotari replies. "Once its artificial intelligence program evolves, it will."

"But I will never give you the invocation," Kun declares.

"The program *will* include the Nine Hands!" Monotari cries. He barks a command. The Ninjaborg fires a volley of laser darts at Kun.

Kun does the most amazing things to elude them. He flits from tree to tree, his feet never touching the ground, staying a split second ahead of the fusillade. Not only that, Kun is able to fire back thunderbolts of some kind. Without budging, the cyborg just absorbs them—the electricity buzzes around his armor and disappears.

Turn to page 97.

Richard suddenly looks very interested. "Tell me more," he says.

You describe your battle with the black-armored ninja. Nada pulls the glove out of her pocket and hands it to Richard.

"Could be a borg," he says after a quick inspection of the glove. To your blank looks, he explains, "Cyborg, short for cybernetic organism. Similar to a robot, but made of more than just computer chips and mechanical parts. It's probably also got organic memory media, lab-bred flesh, pirated organs, and so on."

"Sounds superhuman. Is there any way to stop it?" asks Nada.

"Sure. Anything can be counterprogrammed," Richard answers in a nonchalant tone. "I'll help you, if you want."

"Great. We can use all the help we can get," you say. Ignoring Nada's doubtful look, you pull the computer printout you found in the vault from your pocket. "What do you make of this?"

He reads over the memo. "Obviously the Acquisitions Department had a reason for letting this Monotari character in here to search your vault. I could try to find out what it is, but I've never had any luck hacking into *their* system before. I can try again, or I could beam out for this Monotari guy in CyberWorld."

"What about the glove?" you ask. "Can you get anything from it?"

Go on to the next page.

"Yes!" Richard exclaims. "If enough of the circuitry's intact, I might be able to extract the machine code. That's kind of like the DNA of the borg—it'd tell us a lot about the thing."

"Why not do all three?" Nada demands. "Then we can track down the borg, Monotari, the Acquisitions Department, or whoever. I just want to know where the scroll is and what it's being used for."

Turn to page 92.

Nada shakes the facsimile of the scroll, still warm from the printer, at Richard. "This is just a copy! The paper hasn't been made from the trees of my ancestors! It doesn't hold the sweat and fingerprints of the sage who wrote it! It doesn't smell of the Vault of Scrolls!"

"Cool your spool," Richard retorts, disappearing behind the Vizard. "Okay, I'll tell you where it came from. I got it out of this guy Monotari's files. The one who left behind the memo. He lives in some big castle. He's an artificer—that means he constructs cyborgs and other critters."

"What was he doing with the scroll?" you ask.

Richard keeps moving his mouse around and typing. "It looks like he was putting it into . . . some kind of artificial intelligence program . . . for something called . . . the Ninjaborg."

"The Ninjaborg," Nada repeats quietly. "That must have been the robot that came back in time to steal the scroll." Her voice rises an octave. "And now they're trying to program the Nine Hands into a cyborg! We've got to stop them!"

Go on to the next page.

"It's too late. If this information is already on the database, it's got to be in that cyborg," Richard informs her. Before Nada can have another outburst, he says, "But hold on. For some reason, it hasn't worked. Apparently there's a second part to it, some kind of code that allows the data in the scroll to be activated. Monotari can't find it."

"Hmmm," says Nada. "Kun never mentioned that. But there could be a spoken part, a *Kuji* invocation that's never been written down."

"Risky form of data storage," Richard comments.

Turn to page 57.

You place the glove before Kun. He squints and holds the jewel closer to his eye, then farther away. "It's very cloudy," he announces at last. "There's a great miasma. This object comes from, I'd say, oh, about fifty years into the future. But that's all I can discern."

"It's obvious, then," Nada declares. "We must travel to the future ourselves. Kun, you can do this? You can use *saiminjutsu* to send us forward in time?"

"Yes," he answers slowly, "but . . ."

You shiver involuntarily. "I don't know if this is such a good idea. What if all the ninja are as creepy—and as strong—as the one that was here? This future doesn't sound so great."

"You're right to be cautious," Kun agrees. "It's dangerous. Going into the past is dangerous too, but at least you know what to expect. People in the future know more than you do. You are at a great disadvantage. Yes, it's very, very risky."

"Kun, will you come with us?" Nada asks.

Turn to page 3.

"Are you all right?" you ask Nada.

"Yes—I sensed it coming at the last second. It didn't cut far into my skin. But the thing is, even though I felt the *shuriken* coming, I still don't pick up any vibrations from the ninja himself."

"I don't either," you say. "It's like he's got no smell."

"I've never heard of a ninja training himself to give off no vibrations whatever. That's impossible!"

"I've never seen anyone move so fast, either. The guy's *inhuman*."

"No ninja can do that, I don't care how well trained he is," Nada asserts.

And yet he does. You give Nada a long look. The next moment you're diving to the side as you hear a buzz, then a crack that sounds like lightning. You're frozen for a second. A vapor trail left by the lightning hangs in the air in front of you.

Then you hear another crack, followed by splintering wood. Something makes you look up. A very large pine tree is growing larger. It's falling out of the sky and is going to land precisely on the spot where you're lying.

You and Nada scramble out of the way of the plunging tree. Needles whistle by your ears, and cones come bouncing out of the fallen branches. Moments later, you follow the fallen tree back to its trunk. Char marks at its base confirm it was the target of the second lightning bolt.

Turn to page 89.

16

"But what?" you ask. "All we've done is to scare away Monotari and the Ninjaborg for a little while."

A smile spreads across Kun's face. "Ah, yes. But now that we understand their intentions, I can send you back to the time before the Ninjaborg stole the scroll. You can remove it from the vault and put it in a new hiding place. I can't be certain, but this just might take care of the matter once and for all."

Your head is spinning. "But then we'll be re-living our lives before the time when the Ninjaborg came . . ."

You look at Nada, who's just as puzzled. Kun gives an enigmatic smile. At least *he's* enjoying this. "Don't worry. It will all work out, you'll see. As the two times converge, you will lose your memory of this event. If another time comes when it will be of use to you, it will reappear as a déjà vu. Or perhaps you will pass it along to your children as a fairy tale. This is the way with *saiminjutsu*."

You can only shake your head, perplexed.

"It's time for you to go now," Kun says. "Monotari and that creature will be back before long, and I must hide. But first, I will return you to a time a little before your own."

Kun instructs Nada where to hide the scroll when she returns. Then he has you sit in meditation. He seems rushed as he begins the *saiminjutsu* trance. The last thing you hear is leaves rustling a little way off.

Turn to page 23.

It is the Ninjaborg itself. It fills the space with its gleaming layers of black armor and its implacable, dark-visored face. Once again you sense no presence from it, which is the most frightening thing of all.

Richard, however, is paying no attention to it. He's busily working at his handheld computer. Suddenly a buzzing comes up the corridor behind Monotari. You turn and see the rest of the swarm formed into a grid barrier, advancing on him, pushing him toward you.

"Aaugh! I hate bugs!" Monotari screams. The Ninjaborg springs into action.

"Split up!" you cry to Nada, reasoning that it's your only chance against the machine. You duck into a passageway to your right as the Ninjaborg comes for you. Half of you hopes it will follow you, giving Nada and Richard a chance to deal with Monotari. But the other half knows that if it does, this could be your last ninja battle.

It does. You hear it behind you as you tear down the passageway. Thankfully you come to a heavy door, which you slam shut and bolt. Seconds later, you hear wood splintering as the borg attacks the door. You run up a narrow staircase.

The stairs climb higher and higher. Gasping for breath, you fling anything you can find down the stairs behind you—old suits of armor, chairs, window shutters. You know that behind you somewhere is the Ninjaborg, silently gaining ground. And it doesn't get winded.

Turn to page 70.

18

You're confused. "The ninja is a *spirit*?"

"Hardly," Kun replies dryly. "After all, he's not dead yet! Besides, if he were a *kami,* I would have gotten a much stronger sense of his presence. No, this is an entirely different creature. Its nature is beyond me."

"It's like a robot or something," Nada says.

"Right!" you agree. "If it's from the future, it could be some kind of computerized ninja."

Kun shakes his head in disgust. "Absurd. All of the arts of ninjutsu are intuitive—exactly the opposite of a computer."

"It *would* explain how he could move with such speed. And the circuitry in the glove. And the plasticized finger," you point out.

Now Kun looks downcast. He doesn't like hearing all these terms he doesn't understand. But his face brightens and he puts a finger in the air. "Wait, I know! I will consult the jewel. Go to the main house and wait for me there."

You and Nada start back up the path while Kun goes flitting through the woods to retrieve his jewel. A few minutes later he comes prancing back into the living room of the house. In his hand is a diamond the size of a golf ball.

"This is the Jewel of Re," Kun explains, setting it on a low table. "It was given to me by a *tengu* I knew long ago. Through it I can see a thousand years into the past. But I can also see a thousand years into the future!" He snaps his fingers. "Bring me the glove."

Turn to page 13.

Richard relays his findings. "No big surprise here. The Acquisitions Department's been funding this thing. What I don't get is why they're letting Monotari keep it." The keyboard pitter-patters, and Richard says, "I'm getting out of this guy's reality before he beams in. Now we're back in Curtel. Let's see what we can find."

After several more minutes of pattering and clicking, Richard announces, "Here we go. A memo circulating in Curtel says Monotari is withholding company property—i.e., the Ninjaborg. The Acquisitions Department financed the project and now they want the fruits. They're sending a repo officer out to confiscate it."

"When?" Nada asks. "I'm worried they'll take the scroll, too."

"You should be," Richard remarks. "If they swallow it up, you'll have a hard time getting it back." He does more work on the computer and says, "Sorry. That's all the information I can get right now. I'd have to hack into the Acquisitions Department for more. I've never been able to do that before, but I can try."

"How can it hurt?" you ask.

Richard lifts the Vizard. His brown eyes seem vulnerable as they readjust to daylight. "With the Acquisitions Department, you never know. It could blow our cover. They could detect our inquiries, home in on our transmittal quadrant, and come looking for us."

Go on to the next page.

"Sounds like it might not be worth the risk," Nada says. "We know where Monotari is—let's get started."

"Monotari's castle won't exactly be risk-free," Richard adds. "And besides, maybe Curtel has already located the borg. Only classified Acquisitions Department files would show whether the repo guy has come up with anything. That is, *if* we can access them." Richard looks worriedly up at you.

Nada does too. "What do you think?"

*If you tell Richard to hack away,
turn to page 73.*

*If you decide not to risk it and head out for
the castle, turn to page 102.*

You rub your eyes and sit up. You're in the same place, but it's different. The clearing is larger, and the trees are greener. The sky seems bluer, too. You look at Nada and say, "Well, I guess we made it."

"Let's get right to the vault," she says. "We don't know how far ahead in time of the Ninjaborg we are."

You run to the vault where, to your relief, you find the Scroll of Nine Hands safely in its place. Nada phones her cousin Saito and a little later he rides up on his motorcycle and takes the scroll away to the hiding place Kun suggested.

While you watch, you can't stop thinking about Kun. He's more mysterious and amazing to you than you ever imagined. Finally you say, "Nada, who—or what—is Kun really?"

Nada can't prevent a little smile from showing on her face. "He's a character, isn't he? I never quite believed it before, but they say he's taught generations of ninja."

"I guess that doesn't surprise me," you say.

Nada lowers her voice. "Some say he's a *tengu*."

Your jaw drops. The *tengu* are mythical creatures who are supposed to have taught the ninja their art. You thought they only existed in ancient times. But after all you've seen, it's not hard to believe there's one right close by.

The End

You had thought the greatest challenge during your two weeks here in the mountain retreat would be to overcome your own restlessness. But now you and Nada face a formidable opponent.

The visitor seems not only invincible but untraceable. You're haunted by your glimpse of his shiny black carapace of armor. He looked like some incredibly powerful insect—maybe he really *was* an alien. Worse than perceiving *sakki,* the force of the killer, from him was that you perceived *nothing at all.* What is this new ninja? Where did he get his powers?

Nada is having the same thoughts. "Let's go for a walk," she says. "Maybe we'll find some clues. Or get some ideas."

She's still limping as you follow her to the door, but you're not surprised Nada wants to go out. She's never let an injury stop her before.

Once again the woods seem tranquil. Aside from the bandage on Nada's thigh, it's as if nothing ever happened. Except that now an irreplaceable text from the Vault of Scrolls is missing. You ask Nada to tell you more about it.

"It's called the Scroll of Nine Hands," she answers. "The Nine Hands is a language of transformation. They're mystic hand symbols that tap into the basic patterns of the universe. When used by a practitioner who knows how to channel energy through meditation and *saiminjutsu* —ninja hypnotism—they can unlock forces of great power."

Turn to page 82.

"I've got a feeling we shouldn't go down to the house just yet," you say to Nada. "Let's look around the grounds first."

Nada gives one last look at the house, then goes along with you to reconnoiter the rest of the compound. The other buildings are for the most part locked, so you leave them and begin a survey of the surrounding paths and gardens.

In a dense grove of trees, you think you hear a yelp from down the hill. You look at Nada. "I heard it, too," she says. "Let's move cautiously —use *ko ashi.*"

Ko ashi, meaning "small step," is one of the many techniques of stealth you have learned in your ninja training. Keeping your hips low, you point your front foot down the hill and use a short, stabbing motion to slide it under the leaves on the ground. Then you lift your rear foot, glide it forward until the toe is pointed ahead, and it becomes the front foot. An observer might think you resembled a crane.

Moving this way, you and Nada are able to silently approach a clearing in the trees below you. But you are not prepared for what you see from your hiding place in the leaves.

About fifteen feet away from you is a man sheathed from head to toe in a nonreflecting black latex ninja suit. Only his face is exposed, revealing harsh features fixated on something ten feet away from him. Closer to you is the armor-plated back and helmet of the ninja that invaded the vault. He's staring at the same spot.

Turn to page 41.

"Let's check out the other clues first," you say. "We can always do the global search later if we strike out on Monotari and the glove."

"Good program," Richard agrees. "I'll teach you how to beam into CyberWorld so you can hunt around for Monotari. Then Nada and I will dissect the glove."

"Why do you call it 'beaming in'?" you ask Richard as he hands you the Vizard.

"Watch. *On*," he commands the computer. As the machine reboots, you notice an array of laser beams going from a lens below the screen into the visor. "The computer receives the cellwave through the modem, then digitally converts it to laser optics, which in turn are beamed to the Vizard."

When you put on the visor, the flat, on-screen representation of CyberWorld becomes holographic. "Cool."

"*Hyper*," Richard corrects you. He shows you how to navigate your way through CyberWorld, then leaves you to search for Monotari's computer address on your own.

You use the mouse to walk your Visitor through the high-rise canyons of CyberWorld. Every once in a while you stop to click open a door and listen in on an electronic conversation. You hear Vizards discussing everything from the latest weather wars—battles between artificially induced tornados, hurricanes, and thunderstorms—to a TV pet gene-splicing contest to produce "America's Funniest Home Mutants."

Turn to page 56.

You turn in astonishment to Nada. "Is it a ghost? I thought you said Kun was—"

"No one ever said he was *dead*," Nada points out. "We just hadn't seen him for a while."

"I've been around all right," Kun agrees with a decisive nod. "For longer than you might think!"

"To what do we owe the honor of your company?" Nada asks.

Kun looks at you. "I have come simply to answer your important question. You asked if the Scroll of Nine Hands can be used for evil purposes. Unfortunately, the answer is yes. *Kuji* has a very powerful effect on the adept. The greater a ninja's mastery, the greater the temptation to use it for personal profit."

"Do you know who stole the scroll?" you ask.

Kun's face freezes. He looks at the ground for a moment. "I have never before encountered anything like it. I know every single animal, every insect, on this mountain, and yet I barely detected his presence. That's why I didn't arrive in time to help you defend the vault. But if I had, I doubt even I could have stopped him."

Nada looks worried. "What do we do, then?"

Kun shrugs. "Tell me what you know about him."

Turn to page 35.

Nada sets the glove on a rock and gently squeezes the severed digit from its black casing. More green and white jelly oozes out, followed by a pale lump. It sits on the rock like a grayish-white slug. You poke at it.

"It feels like rubber or something," Nada says.

You peer at the bottom of the cut-off finger. "Look, there's tiny wires and electrodes running through it."

"We were right. This thing isn't human," she declares.

You inspect the glove. It's flexible, like leather, but much tougher. It's made of a synthetic material you've never encountered before. "There are wires in the glove, too. And tiny electronics inside—circuitry and stuff. It looks like the inside of my computer."

Nada scratches her head. "That might explain how he broke through the door to the vault so quickly. The lock has all these tiny, precise burn holes through it, as though they were made by a laser. I've never seen anything like it in this world."

"What are you saying—we've been robbed by a ninja *alien?*"

Nada sighs. "I don't know. All I know is that he took our most ancient, valuable scroll. It can't be replaced. The stuff in it is so secret and powerful it wasn't written down anywhere else. He knew exactly what he was looking for. Didn't take anything else. Didn't even make a mess."

Turn to page 98.

You put on the Vizard. While Richard operates the keyboard of the computer, laser images appear before your eyes. The first is a menu of video games—"Robo Venge," "Pod Hunt," and "Kill Zone." Richard clicks off the menu, explaining, "Those are for zombvids. You need motor coordination, but no brains. To do some real travel, you've got to beam into Cyber-World."

Richard taps keys. Suddenly the scene goes holographic. You enter a realm of brightly colored geometric buildings. Neon signs identifying each building recede into three-dimensional space. Richard puts your hand on a mouse and has you move it forward. A little electronic person starts walking down the avenue between the buildings. "That's your Visitor," Richard says. "Like in the old days when the cursor showed you where you were on the screen, the Visitor shows you where you are in CyberWorld."

You read the signs on the holographic buildings aloud. "Hyper Reality Club. Media Victims Anonymous. Star Trek, the 24th Generation. Metatron, the Recording Angel."

Turn to page 68.

"Okay, let's follow the insect things," you say to Nada.

You run down the hill to the front door of the main house. It's barred. Nada has you stand back and proceeds to take out her frustrations of the past few hours on the door with a well-placed kick.

The door swings open. The two of you burst in, only to be confronted with a wall of the buzzing creatures. They form a grid barrier that blocks your way into the living room. The room beyond them is empty except for a low table. A keyboard and large computer screen are on top of the table. And seated on a pillow behind it is a young brown-haired guy with a dark visor wrapped around his face. He says, "I'd stop right there if I were you."

Go on to the next page.

Go on to the next page.

"Who are you?" Nada demands sharply.

The guy slowly lifts the visor from his head. "My flesh name is Richard. But if you think I'm going to give you my cybercode, you're crazy. Now you'd better explain what you're doing here. Otherwise I'll relay a command to my swarm that'll make killer bees look like a mosquito picnic."

"We don't intend to harm you," Nada says quietly. "The reason we're here is that this house belongs to my family."

Richard gives a short series of whistles, and the insect things drop out of your way and settle into a corner of the room. "Oh. Well, sorry," he says. "Since the Acquisitions Department closed off access to this whole area, I figured no one used it anymore. It looked abandoned."

"I guess it is," Nada murmurs as the two of you venture into the room.

Richard looks a little older than you. He's got pale skin and thin arms. From the way he squints at you, he must be nearsighted. He doesn't stand to greet you, so you sit down across the table from him and introduce yourselves.

Turn to page 6.

You and Nada outline the little you know: he seemed inhuman; he was so powerful you could not challenge him directly; and he left behind a mysterious high-tech glove.

Kun nods and says, "I have only one thing to add." His eyes take on a sparkle. "I know that you have encountered *kami*—spirits from the past—before. This one is different. This one is from the *future*." He beams with delight in revealing his discovery.

Turn to page 18.

Tanaka pushes at the vault door. "What is the password? Open it."

"Forget it!" Nada replies. "I've never heard of the Acquisitions Department."

"You *will*," the repo man responds impatiently. "One of our properties was recently traced to your time-space coordinates. *WHERE IS IT?*"

"How should I know?" Nada bursts out. "We hardly got a glimpse of the thing!"

Tanaka plucks the paper crisply from her hand. "I am authorized to repossess. You will provide support."

He snaps the briefcase shut and marches down the hill to the main house. You and Nada give each other a stunned look before you follow. You find Tanaka methodically searching the rooms. He discovers the black glove and holds it up with a pair of tweezers. "This is property of the Acquisitions Department. I hereby take possession."

He drops it into a plastic bag that he deposits in the briefcase. Then he marches past you, back into the living room, where he clears a space on the table. "This will serve as my office. However, I will require a chair. I do not wish to sit on the floor."

Turn to page 66.

Richard reluctantly takes off. Before long you're speeding back to the Kurayama mountain compound. As soon as you land, Nada tells you to prepare to return to your own time right away. "Who knows, Monotari may have some way of tracking us back here."

Suddenly Richard looks very sad. "I wish you didn't have to go. I was enjoying the company."

"You've still got CyberWorld," you remind him.

"Somehow it's not the same," he says wistfully.

Nada gives him a kiss. "Take care of the place."

"Maybe someday your family will get to come back."

"I'll leave instructions for them," Nada says, giving Richard a big smile, "to let you—and the swarm—have your own room."

The End

You and Nada dash out the door after the black flash. "It was headed up the hill, toward the library," you say.

As the glass door entrance to the library comes into view, you see a puff of smoke from the outcrop of white rocks above the building. The sound of rocks scraping against one another follows.

Nada looks stricken. "The Vault of Scrolls," she whispers. "It's built into those rocks."

You run after her, circling the library to a stony slope that leads to the white rocks. For the first time you notice a wood lintel over a dark opening in the rocks. It must be the entrance to the Vault of Scrolls. You see no sign of activity there.

Nada approaches the entrance in a crouch. Suddenly she rolls, as if avoiding an attack. At the same moment you hear a sharp *whoosh* of air. Nada lets out a small cry and grabs her leg. You see a dark stain of blood on her *gi* spreading under her fingers.

"*Shuriken!*" she whispers. "It's a ninja."

Again you catch a flash of black. It disappears behind the far corner of the library.

Turn to page 14.

But now you're leaving your stupid mind behind. Not only has it finally shut up, your body feels perfectly in tune. You feel as if it's humming with the natural world around you. You're really listening now, and not just through your ears.

It's taken you a long time to realize that this kind of listening is the heart of ninjutsu. Learning the kicks and punches and special techniques of stealth, invisibility, and combat has been great. But ninja get their real power from being fully attuned to the world around them.

And—there it is again. That strange feeling. It's not as if you're hearing something. It's more like the *absence* of something. Have the birds stopped singing?

Maybe you're listening so closely that you sense the ghost of Kun. He's the legendary sensei who is said to have lived on this mountain for over a hundred years, maybe even two hundred. He trained generations of ninja here. No one knows what happened to him. He must have died many years ago, yet his body was never found.

Then you think you hear a clink. It's just a tiny little plink from somewhere down the hill. Now you're out of your trance, fully awake.

Turn to page 52.

The focus of their gaze is a tiny, bent figure perched in the limbs of a tree—it's Kun!

A series of shrieks comes from the treetops in back of the two ninja. You jerk your head to look, but the others don't.

"Your tricks won't work on us, Kun," the latexed ninja says, making you realize the shrieks were only Kun projecting his voice. "You can't escape. You'll tell us how to unlock the secret of the scroll before this day's over. One way or another."

Kun chuckles from his perch. "You are so sure of yourself, Monotari. A true ninja does not speak in such a manner. He knows the elusive nature of words. You've lost your powers. You had to go and invent your ninja machine to defeat *me*—an old man! Ha ha!"

Monotari clenches his teeth. "The Ninjaborg is the ultimate fighting force. It will be the most powerful ninja the world has ever seen—once I have programmed the Nine Hands into its circuits!"

"Ah yes, but the Scroll of Nine Hands is useless without the *kuji* invocation," Kun taunts. "It's not written anywhere. Even if it was, your machine would never be able to utter it properly. The latent powers of the brain will always exceed technology. We are connected to forces that no amount of terabytes can access."

You glance at the cyborg, which stands impassively as its merits are discussed. As before, you pick up no sensations from it.

Turn to page 7.

Richard spends several minutes reading the data his swarm sends back. "It looks like you're right. The security system is almost entirely automated. If I can program my swarm to distract it for a while, we can open a hole and sneak through."

After a few more minutes on the computer, Richard moves the PTV in very close to the castle. He switches it into chopper mode, hovers, then makes a sudden dash just above the tree line. The swarm follows.

The castle is right in front of you now. Richard flies around to what looks like the back and lands on a remote rampart.

"Now it's our turn," Nada says, jumping out of the PTV. While Richard is busy reprogramming his swarm, you and Nada take stock of the ninja tools you've brought along.

The first thing you put to use is a *kaginawa,* a long rope with a grappling hook at the end. Individual silicon insects fly off on separate missions. You swing the grappling hook and let it go in the direction of a drainpipe twenty feet above you. The hook catches, and you climb the rope to a window below the pipe. The window is rusted shut, but you pry it open with a small blade. Soon you're inside the castle.

Dust and cobwebs choke the air in the dank corridor. As Richard, then Nada follow you in, you say, "This wing must be shut down. I don't think anyone's been in here for years."

Turn to page 108.

Later you and Nada go and knock on his door. He won't open it, but you manage to get a few words out of him. They make you realize you have no choice but to give up your search for the Scroll of Nine Hands. Richard is not coming out of the room for a long time, and you have no hope of surviving in the Miasma by yourselves.

Sadly, Nada prepares to utter the incantation Kun gave her to transport you back to your own time. You'll return empty-handed. But the one consolation Kun didn't mention is that all memory of your failed journey will be erased. You will remain mercifully ignorant of the small world of the future.

The End

Richard works late into the night. When you wake up in the morning, you find him slumped on the table. Nada rouses him and says it's time to go. He's bleary-eyed but ready to hit the road. He unplugs a handheld computer from the one on the table, slides it into his pocket, and whistles to his insect swarm.

"Wait a minute," Nada objects as the buzzing swarm follows you out the door. "Do those things have to come with us?"

"They go everywhere I go," Richard declares.

"What are they, anyway?" you ask.

"My Silicon Swarm," he answers. "Each of them is a microprocessor with a built-in transceiver that interfaces with my main computer. Individually the units aren't that powerful, but collectively they're pretty formidable."

Turn to page 86.

You think you notice something flitting about in the woods out of the corner of your eye. But it doesn't give you the same sense of uneasiness as before, and you want to finish learning about the Scroll of Nine Hands from Nada. "So," you ask, "the scroll contains instructions for these nine basic signs?"

"Exactly," Nada replies. "And if it literally falls into the wrong hands, it could spell disaster."

Again, movement in the trees distracts you. But you have one last question. "You said only adepts can channel this power. Wouldn't they be unlikely to use it for evil purposes?"

Nada shrugs. But before she can speak, the fluttering motions become too strong to ignore. As you look around, a tiny old man materializes on the path in front of you. Both you and Nada jump back. You could swear he flew down from the boughs of the pine tree above.

"Kun!" Nada cries.

"Yes, Nada, it is I," the old man responds.

You gape at the figure before you. Kun is barely over four feet tall. He looks so old that you imagine he's shrunk several sizes from his original height. His narrow head and beaked nose are framed by a few strands of hair coming down from his ears and a long, wispy beard and mustache. His cheeks are bony, and his skin is discolored with spots from the sun. But his eyes are lively with wit and amusement. He has knobby elbows and knees but is obviously still quite agile and, you suspect, strong.

Turn to page 28.

"Okay, let's look at the wetware," Richard says. These are the parts of the borg made up of genetically modified animal parts, cultured tissues, and magnetic-wave plasma. "Look at this. The doctor got his hands on a batch of pirated fetal cells."

"Bleah," is Nada's only comment.

"The software should be the really interesting part," says Richard, changing subdirectories.

Not to you, though. Screens full of machine code and bitmap flash in front of you. You can tell by Richard's silence that he's transfixed.

"Whew!" he says at last. "That's hyper*active*. Monotari has beamed centuries of ninja training and wisdom into the borg's programming. And guess what's the crowning piece of data."

"The Scroll of Nine Hands," Nada laments.

"But," Richard adds, "Monotari hasn't been able to activate it. Apparently there's a second part to it he doesn't have yet."

"Then it's not too late. We still have a chance against the Ninjaborg. Where do they live?" Nada demands.

"In a big fat castle in Nara," Richard says.

Nada jumps to her feet. "Let's go, then."

"Hold on," Richard says. "We've got to check out the Finance files first. A lot of expensive ware went into this borg. I want to know who paid for it."

Nada sits and impatiently drums her fingers.

Turn to page 20.

A hologram of the globe appears. A web of network lines shrink-wraps it and labels the quadrants. "You can call up the vital information about any quadrant on earth, even get a live satellite picture of what's happening there. All courtesy of Small World Marketing Research," Richard says. "Let's try southern California."

A moment later you're watching Comsat relay video pictures of kids free-floating in the air above a big circular machine of some kind at Disneyland. The pictures are so good you can read the name of the ride: The Anti-Gravity Field. The light is a murky gray-brown. In the background, plumes of black smoke rise into the sky. "Ah, the eternal twilight of LA," Richard sighs in mock yearning.

"I guess it's a small world after all," Nada comments. "But isn't CyberWorld just another form of escape, like Disneyland?"

"It's the only one I've *got*," Richard replies testily. Abruptly he barks, "Off," which powers down the computer. "Okay, I've dumped enough data on you. Now you tell me some things. Like, what caused you to jump fifty years into our wonderful future?"

Nada explains about ninjutsu and *kuji*, finishing with the theft of the Scroll of Nine Hands.

"Ah. Sounds like a statistically significant data piracy," Richard comments. "Who stole this scroll?"

Nada shrugs. "That's what we're here to find out. We think it was a robot or something."

Turn to page 8.

50

While the borg is computing, you are too. One last piece of information clicks in for you. There's been a pattern in the borg's attacks. While its ninjutsu is flawless and lightning quick, it's also predictable. Obviously its artificial intelligence program hasn't developed enough yet to adjust its tactics to each opponent. It just keeps using the same tactics over and over again.

So you're ready when it finally decides to stop processing your nonsense syllables and make its next move. As you expect, it feints right, then comes in with a foot-strike from the left. You sidestep it, pivot, and swing the *kusari-fundo*. The borg is exactly where you expect it to be.

The weighted end of the chain smashes the Ninjaborg's visor to pieces. Unable to process its coordinates, it lunges at you blindly, crashing into the walls of the parapet from one side to the other. You easily elude it. Its visage is now nothing but a useless video lens.

You waste no time dashing back down the stairs and through the passageway. A few of Richard's insects are buzzing around in the hallway. You follow them until they bring you to a cybernetic laboratory. There Nada and Richard have Monotari tied into a chair with the *kaginawa*. The swarm buzzes around him.

He stares at you in utter shock. "How—how could you possibly escape?! Where is the Ninjaborg?"

"He's playing pinball with himself up on a parapet," you answer.

Turn to page 115.

52

You shift your eyes in Nada's direction. She hasn't moved a hair for the past half hour. Apparently *she* doesn't sense it, but your feeling that things are awry is overwhelming.

You listen again. For a moment, you imagine you hear a distant motorcycle. It's gone quickly, though.

You try to tune into *sakki*—a kind of inner radar that senses "the force of the killer." If someone is threatening you or the Kurayama clan, you should be able to pick up on his harmful intentions.

But you pick up nothing. What if this is all just a trick of your mind?

You want very badly to break the silence of the moment and check in with Nada. The problem is, you and Nada have pledged to speak as little as possible during your retreat, especially during meditation time. You're afraid that if you speak up, it will betray your lack of enlightenment—or even worse, it will show weakness. You'd lose face.

On the other hand, you're supposed to be able to trust your own instincts. And they are screaming at you to say something.

If you decide to speak, turn to page 5.

If you remain silent, turn to page 104.

Although you hate the idea of seeing the future before its time, you resign yourself to your fate. "All right, let's do it," you say to Nada and Kun. "It looks like a trip to the future is our only chance to get back the Scroll of Nine Hands."

Kun gives a single nod. "I will get ready for the *saiminjutsu* ceremony. Meanwhile, you must prepare yourselves for an uncertain environment. Wear simple clothes so you will not stand out. Take only a few tools of ninjutsu you can keep easily concealed. And don't forget to take the black glove with you, too. It might help you find the ninja."

An hour later you meet back in the small meditation pagoda. Kun has changed into a ceremonial kimono. You and Nada are wearing plain dark shirts, jackets, and pants. Your jackets are lined with secret pockets for ninja tools.

Kun has you sit cross-legged in front of him. Then he instructs, "First we must meditate together until our minds are linked by subtle vibration."

After a period of meditation, Kun stands in front of you. A surprising intensity comes into his lively eyes. You find yourself staring into them, becoming lost. They look like deep wells. You feel yourself falling.

Kun counts down in a slow, mesmerizing voice. "Ten, nine, eight, seven . . ."

The last thing you see is Kun twisting his fingers into a mystic *kuji* sign. Then all goes black.

Turn to page 100.

Monotari makes a sudden grab for Nada as she is getting back to her feet. You raise the jewel, catching a glimpse of Nada delivering a snap kick to Monotari's knee. As he crumples, the jewel comes to life. A spinning prism of light radiates from its facets. It spins faster and faster until the spectrum envelops everyone in the clearing. A glance at Kun tells you the source is his eyes.

The light is spinning so fast and luminously you have to look away. When it slows down, the Ninjaborg is immobile. Somehow the prismatic light has crashed its circuits. Now Monotari backs away as Nada advances. He punches furiously at a remote control. The Ninjaborg follows him in jerky, awkward movements.

Abruptly, the rotating lights stop. "Let them go," Kun calls to Nada, who is about to catch Monotari. "The creature will regain its powers soon. We have to act quickly."

Turn to page 81.

Another conversation you listen to concerns the nature of Metatron. It seems to be a kind of computer deity, the ultimate artificial intelligence. The cult of Metatron believes that with all the world's computers networked together, the system is developing a consciousness of its own —Metatron. The sheer volume of information traveling through the circuits makes it impossible for any mere human to comprehend the big picture. But Metatron can.

You decide you've done enough random walking. You pull up a menu and look for headings under Ninja. The number of entries astounds you, and you realize something terrible has happened to the concept of ninjutsu.

SERVICES: **Ninja Babysitters, Stealth Savings, Shuriken Carpet Cleaners, Pizza Ninja . . .**

You better not tell Nada about this, you think. She's depressed enough already. Another heading catches your eye: **Ninja Robotics.** You click in and surf through a few entries, but none mention Monotari. An electronic bulletin board looks interesting. You click on it and scan the entire thing. There are posters for robot-warrior bouts, ads for in vitro organ farms, and cards for programming services and virus prevention.

Then you see a tiny notice posted at the bottom of the board: "Seeking spare parts, memory media, tissue cultures. Dr. Monotari. Leave message in mailbox Mono@Mono. $7D^3F4^\pi R^2.X\backslash K$."

"Richard! Nada!" you call. "I've found him!"

Turn to page 88.

"Where's Monotari's castle?" Nada demands.

"In Nara," Richard responds.

"Ancient ninja territory," Nada murmurs. She grabs your arm. "Let's go. We've got to get the original scroll back."

"Are you crazy?" you object. "That's the future out there. We probably wouldn't even get past the Acquisitions Department laser security field by ourselves."

Richard nods his agreement. You go on, "Look, we've gotten what we came for. It's too bad about the original scroll, but at least now we know the Ninjaborg can't put it into action."

"And you've got a perfectly good copy, besides," Richard points out. He seems to feel his work is unappreciated.

"Maybe we can leave a hint for future generations," you add. "Richard could plant the information in CyberWorld. That way your family would still have a chance of getting it back someday."

"Right," Richard says. "That's a much better idea than getting your hands dirty in the real world."

Nada heaves a big sigh and reluctantly agrees. "All right," she says. "But if I live to see this day, I'm going to get good and dirty in Monotari's castle."

You thank Richard and prepare to return to your own time, relieved to leave behind the shrunken future.

The End

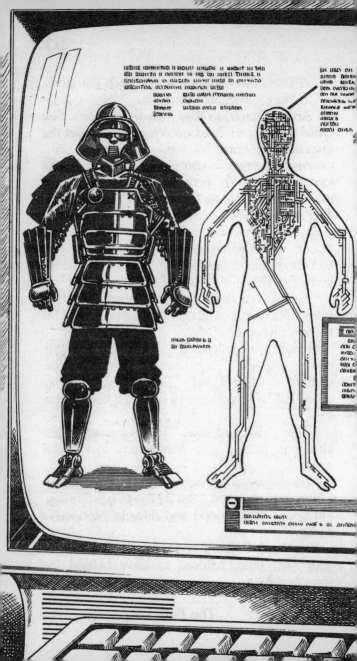

"Man!" he exclaims as diagrams for a complex cyborg scroll down the screen. "You should see this stuff in three dimensions!"

What you and Nada see on the screen is amazing and horrifying enough. Screen after screen of circuitry, mapped out like a huge nervous system, scrolls before your eyes. There are two incredibly complex centers of circuitry and chips, one in the chest of the creature and one in the head.

"The teracomputer in the chest controls the body movements," Richard explains. "The laser rotary encoders enable it to move with inhuman speed. The computer in the head is an artificial intelligence system, including organic memory media. It's a self-modifying information processor—as the feedback loop receives continuing input, it will eventually evolve into an intelligence that even its creator probably can't predict."

The next set of screens shows the Ninjaborg's weaponry. A frightening array of chains, cords, hooks, swords, and *shuriken* is tucked away in its armor. There are also condensers for laser and electric weapons.

The final hardware screens show the borg's skeletal armature, plasticized joints, and tubing. Encasing it all are superhardened plates of armor layered on top of one another like an armadillo's.

Turn to page 48.

You begin a hasty descent from the tree, expecting another precision lightning strike any second. Instead, when you glance up toward the vault, you're blinded by a broad flash of white light. You and Nada shield your eyes.

You move your hand away from your eyes slowly, surprised you are still alive. The white flash was not an attack. All is quiet again except for the faint sound of birds chirping.

"He's gone," Nada says.

Turn to page 74.

Once you're past the Curtel security field and the blades have flattened into wings, Richard speeds the PTV south toward Monotari's castle. Over his shoulder you watch contour maps flash on his flight screen, constantly shifting and adjusting to show your position. They give you confidence he knows where he's going.

Two wind-buffeted hours later, you're approaching a mountain in Nara. Richard hands you a pair of high-tech binoculars and points at a gray protrusion in the rock.

The binocs automatically zoom in on the mountaintop. Hidden among crags and clouds is a castle with turrets and parapets sticking out all over the place. "That must be it," you confirm.

Richard circles it from a safe distance. "Now the question is, what kind of security forces has Monotari got?" he yells back to you. "I'm afraid if I get too close some guard will let loose a shoulder-launched missile."

"I've got a hunch he works alone—people like him are often too paranoid to trust other people," you say.

"Besides, when you've got a force like the Ninjaborg on your side, you don't need a lot of foot soldiers," Nada observes.

"Okay, I'll go in closer," Richard says. "Then I can send out my swarm to do reconnaissance."

He gets out his handheld computer, and suddenly the silicon insects resting quietly around you buzz into action. They fly out of the cockpit and head for the castle in a V-formation.

Turn to page 43.

You rush to help Nada. Her leap apparently broke the time-strobe, because now only she and the Ninjaborg are here, solid, grappling on the ground. And the borg is winning.

You come in with a flying front kick aimed at what looks like a soft spot between the cyborg's neck and shoulders. But his sensors pick you up, and a metal-plated forearm whips a precision block up. You go spinning head over heels down the hill.

You roll to a stop at the feet of Tanaka, who is rushing up the hill, Borgpen in hand. Groggily getting to your feet, you see Tanaka work the switches on the device. The sounds of struggle abruptly cease.

The scene before you is bizarre. The Ninjaborg is frozen in an impossible position, one arm up in the air, the other elbow catching his weight on the ground, along with his hip and foot. It looks as though Nada had just managed to throw him off.

As for Nada, she's lying inert on the ground. You can't tell if she's breathing. "Did the Borgpen freeze Nada, too?" you ask.

Tanaka shrugs. "It may have affected her heart. Once I disable the cyborg, I will release her from the field."

"But she may be dead by then!" you cry.

Tanaka ignores you and approaches the borg. You realize you have only seconds to save Nada.

Turn to page 90.

You peer out the door to see Nada surrounded by a swarm of about a hundred mothlike creatures. From the way they hum, you get the idea they're not actual insects. They keep buzzing her head. Every time she tries to snag one it zips away faster than a fly.

A bunch of them detach from the swarm and buzz over to check you out. They come whizzing in around your ears and arms. You catch glimpses of glassy, multifaceted bodies. Mechanical wings, beating faster than your eye can see, keep them airborne. You try to shoo them away, but they elude your hands and keep up their annoying buzz. Then, abruptly, they all regroup and fly down toward the main house.

"Let's follow them," Nada says, grabbing your arm.

But you resist. You don't like the creepy electronic buzz of the insect things. They seem dangerous and not at all friendly.

"I don't know if we should do that. They might be luring us into a trap. I heard some serious voltage."

Go on to the next page.

Nada stops for a moment. "I guess we could finish looking through the vault and check out the rest of the compound before we approach the main house. But look, they're going inside. Shouldn't we keep them in sight and find out what they're up to?"

You watch the strange swarm crowd through a broken windowpane and enter the house, trying to decide whether to follow them.

If you agree with Nada and go to the house, turn to page 31.

If you tell her you want to check out the rest of the compound first, turn to page 25.

You motion Nada outside while Tanaka busies himself with his briefcase. She's gnashing her teeth. "Can you *believe* this guy?"

"He's got the manners of a camel," you say. "But did you see inside his briefcase? It had some nasty-looking hardware. He's a real pain, but I have a feeling we shouldn't mess with him. After all, he *is* from the future."

Nada folds her arms. "Well, that's obviously where the action is. And it's where we should be. I say we get away from this guy. Leave him to diddle with his briefcase, find Kun, and get out of here."

"But he might be able to help us," you say. "Aside from being totally rude, he's not doing us any harm."

Nada keeps her arms folded. "Maybe, maybe not. Either way, if you ask me, until we plunge ahead into the future, it's going to keep coming headlong at us."

"But Tanaka's *from* the future. He obviously knows more than we do. Why don't we just bite our tongues and see what we can learn from him?"

Nada grinds her teeth and sets her jaw. "Do you *really* want to be on this geek's side?"

*If you say yes,
turn to page 106.*

*If you decide Nada's right and you should
go into the future, turn to page 116.*

"I guess you're right," you say to Nada. "He's going to get into the vault one way or another. There's no point in me getting zapped in the bargain."

Nada gets painfully to her feet. "There's one last thing we can do. It should take him a while to break into the vault. While he's doing that, we can take a long-range shot at him."

You follow Nada down past the library to the small warehouse where a few centuries' worth of ninja weapons and tools are stored. She plucks an ancient crossbow off the wall, hands you some extra arrows, and limps out to a tall pine tree with evenly spaced branches.

"Help me climb," she instructs.

You give Nada a boost into the tree and climb with her until you're high enough to see the white rocks of the vault up the hill. Nada lets out a yelp of surprise when the entrance comes into view. "He's inside already!"

You hand her an arrow. She fits it into the crossbow, draws a bead on the vault opening, and waits. She knows she'll only have a fraction of a second to let her shot go.

Nada doesn't move a muscle, but suddenly the arrow is gone. She lets out a small grunt of satisfaction and puts her hand out for another. Before you can hand it to her, though, another lightning bolt streaks from the vault. It strikes the branch just to Nada's left. The branch shears off and bursts into flame.

Turn to page 60.

Glancing out the edge of the visor, you see that Richard and Nada are watching a simplified version of what you see on the computer screen. "Each of those are what in your day were called user groups," he says. "If you click on the door of, say, Metatron, you'll find yourself in the middle of an electronic conversation with Vizards all over the world who are into the Metatron cult. Your body's here, alone on this mountaintop, but the rest of you is partying down in CyberWorld via cellular uplink."

Suddenly your Visitor bumps into a solid red line. You're at the base of a gigantic pulsing building that now dominates the screen. It stretches farther into the heavens than the Vizard can scale. Above the grand entry door a burning red neon legend proclaims: CURTEL INC. WE'RE MAKING THE WORLD SMALLER.(TM)

"Our old buddies Curtel," Richard murmurs. "I hacked my way into the Marketing Department once. Ooh, it was creepy."

He taps keys for a while, maneuvering your Visitor through schematic hallways to a door that reads MARKETING DEPT. A text line asks for a password. Richard keeps tapping, and a bold logo suddenly fills your vision, followed by a security warning against exactly what you're doing. He quickly bypasses it.

"Check this out," Richard says. "They've got satellites covering every inch of the planet, twenty-four hours a day. At night and in cloud cover they use radar imaging."

Turn to page 49.

The staircase ends at a small door. You go through it and find you are on top of a parapet. Desperately you run to the edge of the battlement and look down. The height makes you dizzy. There's no way off.

You whirl as the door swings open. Now you are face to face with the Ninjaborg. Its blank visor chills your blood.

"Stop!" you command desperately.

"Command Monotari only," the borg responds in a metallic voice; and without further ado, it commences its attack.

You duck and roll out of the way, avoiding the first strike. Two more follow. Reacting purely on instinct, you elude them, too. The borg's gloved fist smashes into the stone of the parapet.

You turn and face the Ninjaborg again. You know you've survived so far only by virtue of anticipation. If you hadn't guessed right on its line of attack all three times, you'd be pulp by now. Lights at the edge of its visor blink, reminding you of the Vizard. It's processing information. That gives you an idea.

The cyborg's language skills seem rather primitive. You utter a string of *kuji* syllables in no particular order. The tactic has the effect you hoped for. The borg recognizes the syllables but can't figure out how to put them together. It pauses, trying to process the information.

This gives you time to extract a *kusari-fundo* from inside your jacket. You utter another string of syllables. Again it pauses to compute.

Turn to page 50.

"You got it," Richard replies grimly. "That's why I had to get out. I control my own input here. Plus the fact I was scheduled for my first hormone-neutralizer injection. They force them on all teenagers, so we'll cause less trouble."

"But aren't you kind of young to be a recluse?" Nada wonders. "Don't you miss being in contact with the real world?"

He gestures at his computer. "Hey, I've got CyberWorld. It's *hyper*real. It's also the only frontier left on the planet. The only place you can escape the Miasma, if you know how to beam in."

To your quizzical look, Richard holds out the visor. "Here, try it. This is a Vizard—a cybermask. You can hide behind it, but it also lets you visit CyberWorld."

Turn to page 30.

Nada offers Tanaka a deal: if he can remove the Scroll of Nine Hands from the Ninjaborg's memory banks and make a hard copy for her, she will release him and allow him to return to his own time.

Tanaka quickly agrees to Nada's offer. You take him back outside to the paralyzed borg. While Tanaka sets to work disabling it, you hold hostage the Borgpen and a time-phase shifter you find in his briefcase.

After a few hours of tinkering, Tanaka holds up a chip. "Here it is. If you will allow me to use the computer in my briefcase, I will print it for you."

Nada keeps a close eye on him while he prints a copy of the scroll. She inspects it closely before announcing, "This is it. A perfect replica."

Tanaka stands up and holds out his hand to you. "Now, if you will permit me . . ."

"Hold on," Nada says. "Give me the chip containing the scroll."

Tanaka reluctantly hands it over. In turn, you hand over the Borgpen and time-phase shifter. "Have a nice trip," you say, backing up very quickly in case he tries anything on you.

But Tanaka has nothing of the sort in mind. He's frantically programming the time-phase shifter.

"Don't forget to take that thing with you," Nada adds, pointing at the borg.

Tanaka and the Ninjaborg are gone in a flash.

The End

"Let's try it," you decide. "We need all the information we can get before we try going anywhere."

"You just never know what they've got up their tube." Richard shrugs and reluctantly dons his Vizard. "Okay. Here goes."

You and Nada watch the screen as Richard sets to work on the computer again. He's already in the Curtel system. He finds his way to the Acquisitions Department easily enough and even manages to get past the security warning.

The number of directories to choose from is so gargantuan you can't begin to read them. Richard notices a special icon in large type called EasyGuide. He clicks on to it. "They make it so convenient," you say.

"I don't like it," he murmurs.

A big logo in large, friendly-looking type fills the screen. "Welcome to the Acquisitions Department," it says. "To begin this guide, click on START."

You sense Richard holding his breath as he clicks on. A smiley face appears on the screen. Its voice comes over the computer speaker. "Are you ready for some fun?"

Turn to page 84.

74

You finish climbing down from the tree and venture up the slope to the outcrop of white rocks. The lintel over the entrance to the Vault of Scrolls has something sticking out of it— Nada's arrow. And something small and black is pinned beneath it.

Nada rushes through the vault's open door. While she surveys the damage inside, you examine the black object pinned to the lintel. It's a glove. When you look closer, you let out a gasp of disgust. The portion of the glove above the arrow shaft is full.

"His finger's still inside!" you cry.

Nada comes out of the vault. She takes one look at the arrow and the glove and says, "I *thought* I nailed him."

Nada works the arrow until she can pull it loose from the lintel. Green and white foam oozes out of the bottom of the glove. You hold it by the edge and turn it upside down so the stuff stops oozing. Then you make a face at Nada and say, "What's *in* here?"

"There's only one way to find out," Nada replies.

Turn to page 29.

"Do the global search," you say to Richard. "Let's let our fingers do the walking."

"All right," Richard agrees. "Give me a couple of hours to set up the program. Then we'll just sit back and see what cycles up."

While you wait, you and Nada search the grounds. You find a place in the woods where it looks like a scuffle took place recently. But there are no other clues. Richard kicks back and reads tattered paperback books that he insists are classics. They have weird titles like *Snow Crash, Neuromancer,* and *Metatron.*

A little way into the second day the computer starts to make beeps. It exclaims, "Eureka!"

Richard rushes to put on the Vizard. "Yes! Yes! We've got it!" he cries. *"Print!"* he commands the computer. A machine on a cart under the table whirs into action.

Before you know it, a perfect laser-printed replica of the Scroll of Nine Hands has emerged from the computer. Richard lifts the visor and peers at it for a moment. Nada grabs it out of his hand. "That's some obscure program code," he remarks.

"It means nothing to the uninitiated," Nada says. "But thanks for tracking it down. Now, where's the original?"

Richard gives Nada a long look before putting the Vizard back on. "What do you need the original for? I got you a hard copy. It's got all the data."

Turn to page 11.

You enter the main house silently. Wordlessly you split up to make a quick, methodical search. When you meet Nada back in the kitchen, you see that she's found the same as you—nothing.

"Maybe I was just imagining things," you mumble.

"No, I'm beginning to see what you mean," Nada says, stroking her chin with her forefinger. "It's almost like everything's *too* perfect, *too* quiet. Yet the air is charged."

You nod. Both of you stand perfectly still for several moments. Every pore in your body is open to pick up vibrations. Not just sound and light, but the many other kinds of invisible vibrations undetectable by scientific instruments. Ninjutsu has taught you that the universe is full of crisscrossing forces. These forces are the stuff of *kuji.*

In your heightened state, the corner of your eye catches a flicker of black outside the window. It goes by faster than your brain can register to turn your head.

"Did you see that?" Nada blurts.

"Yes!" you say. "Something black. It was moving too fast to be human, even a ninja. I thought maybe it was a crow."

"But it was way too big to be a crow, or any kind of bird," Nada replies. "Not only that, it seemed to gleam like metal."

Turn to page 38.

You nod at the jewel. Nada returns your nod, then springs out of the bushes as if shot from a coil. You make a lunge for the jewel.

Nada's aim with the *kusari-gama* is perfect, but it just bounces off the Ninjaborg's hardened metal shell. She manages to pick it up again. The cyborg pivots to face her. But instead of trying to fight it, she ducks under its lightning-fast fist-strike and dives toward Kun, whom Monotari is trying to pin down.

Nada is able to slash twice at the net before taking a blow from the Ninjaborg that sends her flying backward. She drops her weapon. Kun squirms out of Monotari's grip and through the hole in the net. He grabs the blade handle of the *kusari-gama*.

Monotari laughs. "Go ahead, old man. See if you can defeat my creation with your pitiful weapon!"

The Ninjaborg faces Kun and takes a fighting position. Its movements are uncannily precise and fast—almost too good to be believed. But Kun does not intend to take up Monotari's challenge. Instead, he holds the blade to his own throat.

"I may not be able to defeat your creation, but I can defeat your purpose," Kun says. "My time has nearly come anyway, Monotari. I would not be sorry to go this very minute."

Monotari looks panicked. Kun shifts a quick glance to you and sees the jewel. With an upward flick of his eyes, he instructs you to raise it.

Turn to page 55.

You wander back outside to the Vault of Scrolls, where Nada is busying herself looking for clues, though you've already been over it twice with a fine-tooth comb and found nothing. You fill her in on what you've learned.

Suddenly you hear a series of loud electrical discharges outside. You and Nada rush to the door. Immediately you must protect your eyes from a burst of bright flashes. The flashes come faster and faster until they are pulsing like a strobe light. As your eyes adjust, you catch a glimpse of three figures phasing in and out of existence. The first is a man in black ninja garb. The second is the armor-plated Ninjaborg. And the third is very small and floats above the ground—it's Kun!

He seems to be locked in a standoff with the two ninja. But because they're all phasing in and out of being here and being in the future, they can't break it.

"I've got to save Kun!" Nada cries, preparing to jump into the fray.

"Nada—no!" you scream. But it's too late. She leaps into the time-strobe field.

You catch freeze-frame glimpses of what happens next. In one frame, Nada is flying underneath Kun, who is now ten feet off the ground. In the next, she's about to run into the Ninjaborg. In the third, the cyborg is wrestling her to the ground.

Turn to page 62.

Once you've caught your breath, you and Nada sit down in the clearing with Kun. You regard him with amazement. Yes, he looks older and more feeble than when you first met him. But how can he still be alive fifty years in the future?!

Kun tells you what he knows. Monotari is a scientist who grew up in a ninja clan. But he wasn't satisfied with the way the powers of ninjutsu compared to the growing power of technology. He started working as a scientist for a powerful corporation called Curtel, Inc. But his work deteriorated and before long he lost the respect of both his scientist colleagues and his ninja family. That was when he dedicated himself to a project that would combine both worlds —a ninja cyborg that would give him dominance over all who had rejected him.

Turn to page 94.

"What are these basic patterns of the universe?" you ask Nada.

"Well, the universe is made up of subatomic particles, right? The world looks solid and stable, but at the subatomic level these particles are in a constant state of flux and uncertainty. They divide and recombine all the time. Parallel universes split off from the series of choices that make up the particular universe we inhabit. It's just like when you made the choice to return here to Japan, you left behind the parallel life you could be living in San Francisco."

"Okay," you say. "I'm following you so far."

"Okay, so no matter how stable physical reality may look, the universe actually is in a constant state of flux. *Kuji* is the ninja method of influencing that flux. Some call it sorcery, but really it's just a method of changing the vibratory patterns of subatomic particles. A very skilled ninja can even use it to change his own shape."

"So what are the Nine Hands—a type of *kuji*?"

Nada takes a deep breath before answering. "They're the key code to all of *kuji*. These nine symbols resonate with the most basic levels of reality. They unleash tremendously powerful vibrations, giving the user the ability to alter the very fabric of reality. Of course, you have to know how to use them. Used by someone without training, they'd look like nothing but a bunch of twisted-up fingers."

Turn to page 47.

"That's okay," Richard continues. "You don't have to give away your transport secret. I'll just accept that you're from the past. You sure *look* like your shelf dates have expired."

"Thanks a lot," Nada retorts. "Now, suppose you explain some things. What's the Acquisitions Department?"

"Who knows, anymore?" he replies. "It used to be part of Curtel, the information and robotics cartel. But it kept acquiring things and outgrew its parent. Then real estate prices tripled, and suddenly it was beyond big. The huger it gets, the more its appetite grows. It just keeps stuffing itself in a self-reinforcing feedback loop."

"So now it owns huge tracts of land that it won't let people pass through?" Nada asks.

"Exactly. They close down mountain areas like this so that you can't escape the Miasma— the wall-to-wall malls, franchises, burbs, parking lots, and traffic jams.

"See, it's all part of the plot to make the world smaller," Richard goes on. "To corner market share. By shrinking the world and making it more interconnected, they have greater control over consumer geography. Their goal is to get every human alive jacked in to relentless media input. They've figured out how to pulse microsignals on a wavelength that hypnotizes the part of the brain responsible for independent choice. Eventually you dope out on mediawave. You turn into a zombvid."

"Video zombie," you guess.

Turn to page 71.

Before your eyes, the face morphs into a smiling clown. The smile gets wider and wider. The features change and redden until it has turned into a hideously grinning demon. And then the grin turns into a glower. The demon's eyes flash. Flames lick out of its nose and ears and finally come bursting through its eyeballs. Now the whole screen is filled with flames.

And then the fire is *real*. The screen starts to buckle and melt. Actual flames lick out of the holes being created.

"Crash and burn!" a demonic voice screams.

The computer itself lets out a final, agonized "AAAAUGH!" before expiring in a burst of crackling sparks. Richard slowly lifts his Vizard and stares at the ruined screen. "Wow," he says in a low, awed voice. "They must have developed a new virus-bomb." His awe disappears as he realizes his most precious possession has just been destroyed. He throws down the visor and bursts into tears. You try to put an arm around him, but he jumps up, runs down the hall, and locks himself in a bedroom.

Turn to page 44.

"They gather and collate data. And they protect me when I need it," Richard goes on. "You watch—they'll come in handy. Besides, I programmed some things I learned from the glove into them last night."

You follow Richard to a tangle of brush behind the woodshed. Hidden under some branches is a contraption resembling a very large insect. As you help him untangle it, he explains, "This is my PTV—personal transport vehicle. It runs on solar-chip batteries and has a range of six hundred miles."

You help him wheel it out to an overgrown driveway. It consists of a small fuselage the size of a roller-coaster car, a tail fin and horizontal stabilizer, and struts supporting a cylinder above the cockpit, which Richard climbs into. You and Nada crowd in behind him. Nada grimaces as the swarm settles in around your feet.

Richard starts the PTV up. A pair of wing-blades unfolds from the cylinder above your head. "Strap in!" he calls back as he buckles a pair of belts crisscrossing his chest. "These are the only things between you and free fall."

The blades rotor like a helicopter. Before you know it, you're above the ground and flying off the top of the mountain. "The Curtel security force field extends two miles into airspace," Richard yells over the noise. "We'll have to stop and open a hole in it. When we're through, I'll put the rotors into wing mode. Then we can really *fly*."

Turn to page 61.

Nada and Richard rush in from the other room, both wearing latex gloves smeared with greenish-white jelly. Richard reads the screen and says, "The X\K extension means you can't just go knocking on his door. You have to have his password to contact him directly."

"So we have to leave a message?" Nada asks.

"Heck no," Richard replies, peeling off his gloves and taking the Vizard back. "That's for zombs. It shouldn't be hard for me to hack up."

Richard succeeds in finding the password, but nothing happens when he calls Monotari's computer address. "No one home," he murmurs. "He's not beamed in. Let's see if I can do a little breaking and entering."

Soon Richard is shuffling through Monotari's files. On the computer screen you and Nada see a version of what Richard has in the Vizard. The more you see, the more you fear seeing. Monotari is a high-level scientist on the payroll of Curtel, Inc. Not only is he a scientist, Richard explains, he's an artificer, which means he constructs cyborgs and other creatures. And, it soon becomes clear, not only is he an artificer, he's also a ninja. "It'll be a nightmare if he's managed to combine the two," you murmur.

Then Richard finds it. A directory called NINJABORG.

"Oh, no," Nada moans softly.

It has subdirectories for Hardware, Software, Wetware, and Finance. "Let's see what this thing looks like," Richard says.

Turn to page 59.

"That's the most incredible weapon I've ever seen," Nada gasps.

You catch yet another glimpse of the intruder racing back up toward the vault. He's visible for only a few seconds, but this time you take in its complete form. What you see astounds you.

"He looks like some kind of knight," you whisper. "He's covered in armor, but it's dark and shiny. It's not like anything I've ever seen. And he moves ridiculously fast, especially for someone wearing so much metal."

Nada grimaces in pain. "It's like he's from another century. And he's obviously after the most precious thing we have here—the ancient scrolls in our vault."

Your glance falls to Nada's thigh, where her hands press against her *shuriken* wound. It's up to you. "I've got to try to stop him. We can't let him break into the vault."

"No!" Nada says sharply, grabbing at your sleeve. "Don't be foolish. He's too strong for us. The tree, the *shuriken*—they were just messages. We have to stay out of his way."

You hesitate. It's obvious you're dealing with a foe who's more powerful than anything you've ever encountered. But the Vault of Scrolls contains the secret wisdom of generations of the Kurayama family. It must be defended at any cost. Centuries of tradition—the entire *ryu*—may be at stake.

If you try to stop the ninja, turn to page 111.

If you stay with Nada, turn to page 67.

Silently you steal up behind Tanaka. He has no idea until the last minute that you are there. A pair of simultaneous, precisely placed finger jabs to his temples deprives him of consciousness. As he crumples to the ground, you take the Borgpen from his hand.

Desperately you scan the control panel. You throw what looks like the main switch. It's like releasing the pause button on a video player. Suddenly everything swings back into action. The Ninjaborg finishes landing on his side. Nada rolls away from him. Then the borg springs to his feet, and you can tell he's processing whether to go after you or Nada.

You flip the switch again. Just as you hoped, the electromagnetic field freezes the Ninjaborg, but by now Nada is far enough away that she's not affected. She staggers over to join you.

"Wow," she moans, holding her head, "I feel like I just got hit by a truck."

"Your eyes are spinning," you say. "You better go inside and lie down."

"Not until we take care of Tanaka," she replies.

Ten minutes later, you and Nada have Tanaka trussed up in the main house. Nada massages his vital points, bringing him back to consciousness. He opens his eyes, shakes his head, and says, "Where am I?"

"Fifty years in the past," Nada answers. "And unless you agree to help us, that's where you're going to be stuck."

Turn to page 72.

"Sure," Richard responds absently to Nada. But you can see he's already hatching another idea. "Or why not let the computer do the work for us? That's what the things were invented for."

You wait. He does some computing in his brain, then goes on, "See, instead of going to the pain of physically searching for these guys, we could have the computer do it. You have to realize that what used to be called the real world, the physical world—it's all been converted to data and beamed up to CyberWorld. Really, there's no need for a body anymore, outside of eyes for the Vizard and hands for the keyboard.

"You just tell me everything you can about this Nine Hand Scroll," Richard adds. "I'll program my computer to run a global search through CyberWorld and any other databases I can hack into. If someone's trying to turn it into machine code, I'll find it."

"You mean," Nada asks, horrified, "somebody might be trying to translate the Scroll of Nine Hands into computer language?"

"Why not?" Richard replies. "If it's as hyper as you say, it could beam deep into the information universe."

Go on to the next page.

He pauses, and his brow furrows. "The only drawback is, CyberWorld's so huge the global search will take some time to run. It'll knock out the computer for a couple of days while it cycles through the stacks. We won't be able to foreground the other clues—like the glove—until the program's done."

Nada looks confused. Richard looks undecided. Both turn to you for a decision.

If you urge Richard to do the global search, turn to page 76.

If you'd rather check out the other clues first, turn to page 27.

"But the cyborg's ninja programming was incomplete without the Scroll of Nine Hands," Kun says. "Monotari must have a new agreement with Curtel, because they gave him permission to come looking for it. He tore the vault apart. Unfortunately, the scroll was already gone."

"What happened to it?" Nada asks.

Kun waves off her question. "That's another story. All I have time to tell you right now is that Monotari sent the Ninjaborg back to your time to get the scroll. But Monotari failed to take into account the missing element—a spoken invocation that has never been written down. When he discovered this, he returned here to try to force it out of me. That's when you arrived."

"And it's a good thing we did!" Nada declares.

"Yes, it is," Kun agrees with a little twinkle in his eye. "However, it's unlikely he could have gotten it out of me. The powers of *kuji* are many, and most of them come from inside. I could have made my brain go dead. Still, who knows what he might have done with my body? You might have seen a Kunborg running around someday!"

"So now we must get back the scroll," Nada says.

Turn to page 107.

Tanaka looks up at you, startled, then taps the words into his computer. "You will tell me more about this later."

You notice a device that was in his briefcase now sitting on the table. It's got a lot of knobs, needles, meters, switches, and several miniature antennae sticking out. "What's that for?"

"It's a Borgpen," Tanaka replies, looking annoyed. "An electromagnetic wave generator that freezes electron flow within its field. It is used to contain and confine cyborgs."

"So you'll use the Borgpen to capture the Ninjaborg?" you persist.

Tanaka squints at data coming up on his computer screen. "Once I analyze its dimensional traces through the space-time continuum, break down its machine language components, and send out a signal to lure it back to these coordinates, yes. I will use the Borgpen to repossess the property.

"Now," Tanaka says, not taking his eyes from the computer screen, "please do not interrupt me further. I will call you when your assistance is required."

Turn to page 80.

Then on Kun's next jump, the borg is too quick. You watch in awe as a compartment in the cyborg's armor flies open and a net shoots out. It catches Kun in midair. He crashes to the ground, entangled. Monotari and the borg advance on him.

You must do something. You see Nada pulling a *kusari-gama*—a blade attached to a chain—from her jacket. She doesn't speak, but you know she expects you to do the same. You have a *kaginawa*—a grappling hook and rope. She nods at Monotari, meaning you should take him. She'll take the cyborg.

You hesitate, and a glint in the grass catches your eye. You grab Nada's arm and look closer.

It's Kun's jewel. Maybe it could help you. It hardly seems an effective weapon for this battle, yet you recall its powers in the past. Should you signal to Nada you're going for it instead of attacking Monotari? Or should you stick to Nada's plan? You have only a split second to decide.

*If you go for the jewel,
turn to page 79.*

*If you get out your kaginawa,
turn to page 110.*

"Wow," you say softly. "We've got to get the scroll back. What can we do?"

Nada hangs her head, shaking it slowly back and forth. "I don't know. He just disappeared in a flash of light. We don't have the first clue where he came from or how to track him down."

She looks up and stares off into the trees. Almost as if making an invocation she adds, "How I wish old Kun were here to help us."

You help her limp back to the main house, carrying the glove and its strange contents. Neither of you speaks. As you clean and dress Nada's wound for her, a terrible feeling of dread descends on you. You have faced many perils together, but the task before you now seems impossible.

You first met Nada when you came to Japan to study aikido at her family's dojo. You didn't realize that hers was actually a ninja clan going back hundreds of years. When an ancient sword caused thunder and lightning to erupt at the dojo, her secret was revealed. You began a crash course in ninjutsu to prepare for the perilous journey you and Nada had to make. Through the powers of *saiminjutsu*—ninja hypnotism— you were able to travel back in time to ancient Japan and solve the mystery of the sword.

Go on to the next page.

You returned to San Francisco, where you resumed your aikido training. But you chanced to meet up with Nada's cousin Saito, and you helped him escape from the *yakuza*—a ruthless band of Japanese gangsters. After that, you decided you just couldn't stay away. You came back to Japan to continue your ninja training with Nada at the Kurayama family dojo.

Turn to page 24.

When your eyes open, you are underneath a pine tree at the mountain compound. But one look tells you it's become a very different place.

A glance at Nada's face confirms the change has not been for the better. Everywhere you look you see evidence of years of neglect. The buildings have fallen into disrepair. The garden has grown wild. Pieces of wood and glass are strewn around.

"What *happened*?" Nada cries in shock.

"I don't know," you reply, "but I have a hunch we should start at the Vault of Scrolls."

You run up the hill. The white rocks are there as before, but the lintel is gone. The inside is a mess, littered with splintered shelves and decaying bits of paper.

"I don't understand how anyone could have allowed this to happen—how *I* could have allowed it!" Nada wails.

"There must be a clue in here somewhere," you say. Nada just stands paralyzed while you poke through the debris.

A scrap of computer printout catches your eye. You pick it up and read, "To: Felix Monotari. From: Acquisitions Department. Re: Permission to pass into Closed Area #217. Use bar code below." Attached to the memo is a plastic strip with a long string of black and white bars.

"Nada, look at this," you say.

But Nada's gone back outside. You suddenly become aware of a strange buzzing sound.

Turn to page 64.

"I don't think we should mess with the Acquisitions Department," you say. "I can't explain it. I just have a feeling."

Richard looks relieved. "That's good enough for me. Let's take off for Monotari's castle in the morning."

"You mean you'd actually venture into the real world with us?" Nada teases.

"What the heck?" Richard shrugs. "It might be fun for a while." He picks up the glove. "Now, we've got the whole evening to see what else we can get out of this thing. Want to help?"

Nada answers Richard's questions about ninjutsu while he feeds code from the chips in the glove into his computer.

Meanwhile, you forage in the kitchen for something to eat. All you find are cartons and cartons of freeze-dried seaweed lasagna. You show them to Nada when she comes in. "I guess this is what he lives on," she says, wrinkling her nose.

Turn to page 45.

You arrive to find a tall, skinny man in dark pants and a white shirt bent over inspecting the laser burn marks in the vault's door. "Who are you?" you ask.

The man ignores you. You step closer. Without standing up or looking at you, he thrusts out a hand, pushes you away, and demands, "Where's the borg?"

At that moment Nada comes running up. "I saw the flash," she says breathlessly. When she sees the guy bent over the door, she demands, "Hey! What are you doing? Get away from there!"

Turn to page 112.

A silly premonition isn't enough to risk breaking Nada's concentration. So, you remain silent and try to focus on your meditation. But that's your whole problem: it's not so much a matter of focusing as it is letting go your mind's desire to be entertained.

You let out a deep sigh. Nada shifts her position slightly. You steal a glance at her, but she's deeply immersed.

The rest of your session is frustrating. You manage to quiet your mind, but it's more like falling asleep than reaching the placid state you seek.

After the session is over, you ask Nada if she noticed anything strange during the afternoon. "No," she says simply, sticking to the vow of silence you're trying to observe.

But you can't help describing the sensations you had in greater detail. "Sometimes when you have a lot of silence around you, you start imagining things," Nada suggests gently.

Dissatisfied, you leave her and make a search of the mountain compound for signs of trouble. But you don't see anything obvious. Nothing turns up during the rest of your stay, either.

Even after you leave, the nagging feeling something has gone wrong never leaves you. You keep wondering about it, but not until years later will you and Nada discover the reason for your premonition. And by then, it's much too late.

The End

106

You try to reason with Nada. "Let's make a temporary alliance with this Tanaka guy. I know he's about as much fun as the stomach flu, but we need him right now as much as he needs us. Maybe he'll explain to us what this is all about."

"Well, you deal with him then," she grumbles. "I'm going back to look through the Vault of Scrolls."

You go back inside and find a chair for Tanaka to sit on. He doesn't bother to thank you. He's already busy picking apart the black glove and the weird artificial finger. He uses surgical instruments to extract tiny memory chips, which he feeds into some kind of analysis drive attached to a computer inside his briefcase.

"We'll do whatever we can to help," you say.

"That is acceptable," Tanaka replies, not looking up.

"What'd you call this thing? A borg?"

"Yes," Tanaka answers absently. "A cyborg. Ninja cyborg, to be accurate. Denoted 'Ninjaborg' by its artificer. The borg was sent here to obtain a certain piece of software from your vault."

"The Scroll of Nine Hands," you say.

Turn to page 95.

"No," Kun replies gravely. "We must let them have it, at least for the time being. I have something else in mind. Besides, they can't put it to use—yet."

"I don't get it," Nada insists. "Fifty years ago you sent us into the future to get the scroll back, yet you knew there was a second part which made it impossible to use."

Kun looks weary as he ponders his answer to Nada. "You see, only by having you come into the future was I able to tell you what I know now. Fifty years ago, I didn't know what to do about this. After the intrusion of the Ninjaborg, I saw only a murky future through the jewel. But I knew something had to be done."

Turn to page 16.

Richard continues to receive readings from the silicon insects on his handheld computer. "Pretty soon I'll be able to tell you how far away any warm-blooded—or cold-blooded—creatures are." He stares at his computer screen, then motions for you to follow him.

Nada lights the way with a flashlight as Richard leads you through musty corridors, down crumbling staircases, and across cold, bare floors. Finally you come to a door that gives onto a lit hallway.

The first sign you have that something is wrong as you proceed down the hallway is the shattered silicon moth you find lying on the floor. "Uh-oh," Richard says. He moves faster, finding another, and then another. "I'm losing my readings," he laments, then tries to punch in a new set of instructions.

A door at the end of the hallway opens, causing all three of you to stop dead in your tracks. A tall figure in black stands there with his arms folded. His voice rings down the corridor. "Did you really think my movement detectors wouldn't pick up your little bugs? And did you really think they could escape the wrath of my creation?"

Go on to the next page.

"Dr. Monotari," Nada says. Monotari gives a slight nod, and she goes on, "I am Nada Kurayama. You have stolen the Scroll of Nine Hands from my family's vault. If you return it to us, we will leave without further trouble."

Monotari gives a dry chuckle. "You will not get it back, nor will you leave." He barks a command and looks over your heads. You all turn to see the figure emerging down the hall behind you.

Turn to page 17.

You pull your *kaginawa* from inside your jacket and prepare for your attack on Monotari and the Ninjaborg. At Nada's signal, you proceed. She springs out of the bushes as if shot from a rifle, making a perfect hit on the cyborg with her *kusari-gama*. You stand up and, with a snap of your wrist, send the *kaginawa* line in Monotari's direction. He sees it coming at the last moment, but he can't do anything about it. It wraps him up, pinning his arms to his chest.

Unfortunately, Nada's attack isn't quite so successful. The blade of her weapon bounces off the borg's superhardened armor and falls harmlessly at his feet. She ducks under the borg's fist-strike, grabs the blade off the ground, and manages to slash an opening in the net in which Kun is trapped before the borg sends her flying with a backhand strike.

You jump in to face the Ninjaborg, desperately trying to come up with a strategy. But your synapses are no match for the precision speed of the borg's programming. You hear a click and with growing alarm see a set of *shuko*—ninja claws—pop out of its fist. And now they are coming at you.

Your evasive move is too late. The *shuko* are the last thing you see, as with uncanny accuracy the cyborg adjusts the aim of his head-strike to finish you off.

The End

"We've got to stop this thing. And right now, while it's preoccupied with the vault, may be our best chance," you say to Nada. "You're injured. You stay here. I'm going to the vault."

"Don't risk a frontal attack," Nada cautions. "If it locks in on you, just get out as fast as you can."

You nod and take off for the vault. You think you have a pretty sound plan in mind. You'll position yourself in the rocks above the entrance and wait for the intruder to come out. From there, you'll be in a good position to smash a rock on its head. If that doesn't work, you can make a quick getaway.

You make it into position and find the biggest rock you can lift. You wait, using meditation techniques to remain alert yet calm.

The moment the black-armored figure emerges from the vault, you let the rock fly. It's a direct hit. The figure collapses to the ground. You start to climb down, thinking he'll be lucky if he's still be alive.

Turn to page 117.

112

The man straightens and looks each of you in the eye. He's got a brush cut, stained buckteeth, and overly long limbs. His white shirt is split by the black stripe of a tie. He seems rather awkward, except that behind his filmy eyes you sense a cold brutality. "Who's in charge here?" he says in a flat tone.

"I am," Nada declares. "And if you don't get away from that door, I'm going to remove you personally."

"I don't recommend it," he says calmly. He opens a black briefcase, pulls out a paper, and shoves it in Nada's face. Then he turns his back on her and resumes his inspection of the door.

You peer over Nada's shoulder. The paper is a memo of authorization. The first thing you notice is that it's dated fifty years in the future.

> To: Hideo Tanaka, Repossession Officer, Curtel, Inc.
> Re: Authorization to secure cybernetic organism project #322.
> Status: At large. To be returned to Acquisitions Department.

Turn to page 36.

114

You shake your head no. "It's too dangerous. We should only travel to the future as a last resort. Besides, I hate the idea of seeing the future. It ruins the suspense. It's like being told the end of a movie before you see it."

Nada looks peeved, but Kun says, "It's certainly a bad idea to go into the future if you are not ready for it. Let's stay right here and see what turns up."

You look at him, awaiting further instructions. He raises his eyebrows. "Well, get to work," he says, shooing you on ahead of him. "I don't have *all* the answers!"

You and Nada spend the rest of the day combing through the vault, the library, the stone hill—anywhere the robot thing was. You dissect the black glove and the bizarre, artificial finger. If there are clues anywhere, you don't know how to interpret them.

Nothing turns up the next morning, either. But in the quiet of midafternoon, that eerie feeling returns—the feeling that a little warp is opening in the fabric of time. You tread warily around the compound, wondering if another ninja robot from the future is about to appear.

You don't actually see the flash. You're down by the woodshed when you catch the reflection of a bright white light on the trees around you. You turn and run up the hill toward the Vault of Scrolls.

Turn to page 103.

Monotari and Richard both give you blank looks, and you have to explain, "It's an ancient mechanical game. You don't need a visor to play it."

Slowly it dawns on Monotari how you managed to defeat his machine. But then he mutters something about a backup system, which makes you say to Nada, "We'd better get out of here before that thing gets its marbles back."

She raises a tattered roll of paper, ecstatic. "I've got the scroll! Let's go."

You and Nada dash through the castle, following Richard and his swarm back to the PTV. You jump in, the swarm settles around your feet, and Richard gets the wing-blades rotoring. Suddenly he looks hesitant and says, "There was some really hyper stuff in there."

"You can come back later," Nada tells him.

Turn to page 37.

116

"Okay," you say, "let's ditch this repo man."

"Good. But first I want to get that glove back. It's the only lead we've got. It might help us find the ninja once we get to the future. I'll go around to the back of the house and start yelling. When Tanaka comes outside to investigate, you slip inside and grab the glove. We'll meet in the woods on the road where we talked to Kun. Got it?"

You nod, and Nada sets off around the back of the house. Her plan works perfectly: after she starts a ruckus, you go in the front door for the glove. It's lying right on top of the table in the living room, next to Tanaka's computer. You grab it and make for the woods.

Five minutes later, Nada meets you there. She makes a series of strange calls. Once again Kun suddenly appears, as if dropping from a tree. Nada explains that an annoying man has come from the future and you're now ready to journey into it if only to get away from him.

"As you wish," Kun says, motioning you to follow him. "Come sit with me in this clearing. I will begin the *saiminjutsu* ritual."

You sit cross-legged in the clearing and meditate for a period of time with Kun. Then he stands in front of you. As you stare into his eyes, you feel yourself becoming lost in them. You don't know what he's doing, but you sense your body starting to free fall.

He begins to count down, "Ten, nine, eight, seven, six . . ." The last thing you see is Kun twisting his fingers into a mystic *kuji* sign.

Turn to page 100.

But you're only halfway down the rock face when he miraculously rises to his feet. You contemplate going in for a finishing blow while he's weakened. But it's soon clear he's hardly been affected by the blow.

He spins in your direction. For a moment you stare him in the face. You see no features, only an inhuman black helmet and blank mirror visor over his eyes. Suddenly you wish you'd been deep enough in your trance to never notice the disturbance.

There's no time to flee back up the rock face —you can only wait in dread for what comes next. In a flash you're incinerated like a bug in a flame.

The End

ABOUT THE AUTHOR

JAY LEIBOLD was born in Denver, Colo., and now lives in San Francisco. This is his fourteenth book in the Choose Your Own Adventure series. Recent titles include *Surf Monkeys, The Search for Aladdin's Lamp,* and *You Are a Millionaire. Ninja Cyborg* is the fourth ninja book he's done. The first three are *Secret of the Ninja, Return of the Ninja,* and *The Lost Ninja.*

Mr. Leibold is also the author of the DOJO RATS series, published by Bantam Books, under the pen name James Raven.

ABOUT THE ILLUSTRATOR

TOM LA PADULA graduated from Parsons School of Design with a BFA and earned his MFA from Syracuse University.

For over a decade Tom has illustrated for national and international magazines, advertising agencies, and publishing houses. Besides his illustrating, Tom is on the faculty of Pratt Institute, where he teaches a class in illustration.

During the spring of 1992, his work was exhibited in the group show "The Art of the Baseball Card" at the Baseball Hall of Fame in Cooperstown, N.Y. In addition, the corporation Johnson & Johnson recently acquired one of Tom's illustrations for its private collection.

Mr. La Padula has illustrated *The Secret of Mystery Hill, The Luckiest Day of Your Life,* and *Secret of the Dolphins* in the Choose Your Own Adventure series. He resides in New Rochelle, N.Y., with his wife, son, and daughter.